LULLABY
BERCEUSE

A WARM PRAIRIE NIGHT

Story & Songs by Connie Kaldor & Carmen Campagne
Illustrations by Brian Deines

Night loves the prairies

When the shadows stretch out
so long on the ground

And even the wild old wind
settles down

It's time to come in,
no time left to play

You can see in the sky
that night's on its way

Night loves the prairies

Willows fade into black,
time seems to have slowed

The dust is too tired
to rise from the road

Night's blanket of stars
will soon cover the sky

And the crickets
will sing you a soft lullaby

Say goodnight to the animals

And all the birds too

Sleep tight little one
for you know I love you

And night loves the prairies

LULLABY
BERCEUSE

All Through the Night

(3:36)

TRADITIONAL, ARRANGEMENT
Connie Kaldor

Sleep my child and peace attend thee
All through the night
Guardian angels God will send thee
All through the night
Soft the drowsy hours are creeping
Hill and vale in slumber steeping
Love alone its watch is keeping
All through the night

While the moon her watch is keeping
All through the night
While the weary world is sleeping
All through the night
Over thy spirit gently stealing
Visions of delight revealing
Breathes a pure and holy feeling
All through the night

Prairie Lullaby

(2:50)

WORDS AND MUSIC
Connie Kaldor

When the sun on the prairie
Is going to sleep
You can see it turn golden
And red in the west
There's the barest of breeze
In the shelterbelt trees
Singing each baby to rest

They sing lullaby, lullaby
Coolies and sloughs
Lullaby, lullaby, coolies and sloughs
The wind and the willows
Will whisper to you
Lullaby, lullaby, coolies and sloughs

When the baby meadowlark's
Fussy and tired
Its mama will cradle it under her wing
She'll call to the winds that blow
In from the west
And this is the song that they sing

Lullaby, Lullaby
(3:12)
WORDS AND MUSIC
Connie Kaldor

Lullaby, lullaby
Baby fuss and baby cry
You'll be sleeping by and by
Sleepy little baby

Things go right
Things go wrong
Hearts can break
But not for long
You will grow up
Big and strong
Sleepy little baby

Lullaby, lullaby
Baby slowly, close your eyes
You'll be sleeping by and by
Sleepy little baby

I Have You
(2:31)
WORDS AND MUSIC
Connie Kaldor

Some have furs
And fancy cars
But I have you, I have you
Some have silk and caviar
But I have you, I have you
Some have emeralds set in gold
But they can't sit and rock and hold you
Like I do, like I do, like I do

Some have lace
And diamonds rings
But I have you, I have you
They always have the latest things
But I have you, I have you
Some are always dressed in style
But they can never catch your smile
Like I do, like I do, like I do

Some have homes
On the finest streets
But I have you, I have you
The finest leather on their feet
But I have you, I have you
Some have wine and a castle keep
But they can't watch you drift asleep
Like I do, like I do, like I do

Dream Baby
L'enfant des rêves

(4:35)
WORDS AND MUSIC
Connie Kaldor,
Carmen Campagne
Based on «Au clair de lune»
(Claude Debussy)

Dream baby
Dream baby
Dream baby dream
Dream baby dream

Close your eyes and dream
There are clouds to cuddle
Moonbeams to climb
Stardust to catch you
Go sailing thru time
Sweetest dreams are waiting for my
Dream baby

Beaux rêves
Fais des beaux rêves
L'enfant des rêves
Fais des beaux rêves

Vol au pays des rêves
Le vent te réchauffe
Les nuages te caressent
La lune te sourit
Les étoiles te chatouillent
Beaux rêves d'enfant
Beaux rêves
C'est l'enfant des rêves

I've Been Told

(1:17)
WORDS AND MUSIC
Connie Kaldor

I've been told the best of dreams
Really can come true
So watch you don't give up your dreams
Like most of the grown ups do
'Cause dreams are there for making up
And waking up to
So go to bed
Lay down your head
And dream up one or two

Hushaby

(3:12)

MUSIC
Connie Kaldor

Bonne nuit

(2:36)

WORDS
Connie Kaldor,
Carmen Campagne,
Marguerite Campagne

MUSIC
Brahms

Bonne nuit cher enfant
Quand tu dors dans mes bras
Le monde tourne en rond
Et le jour reviendra
Jours de larmes

De sourirs
Jours de peines
Ou de joies
Mais ce soir tu t'endors
Comme un ange dans mes bras

La poulette grise

(2:44)

TRADITIONAL, ARRANGEMENT
Connie Kaldor,
Carmen Campagne

C'est la poulette grise
Qui pond dans l'église
Elle va pondre un beau petit coco
Pour son petit qui va faire dodiche
Elle va pondre un beau petit coco
Pour son petit qui va faire dodo
Dodiche dodo

C'est la poulette blanche
Qui pond dans les branches

C'est la poulette noire
Qui pond dans l'armoire

C'est la poulette jaune
Qui pond dans les aulnes

C'est la poulette verte
Qui pond dans les couvertes

C'est la poulette brune
Qui pond dans la lune

Petit bébé

(2:25)

WORDS AND MUSIC
Connie Kaldor,
Carmen Campagne

Petit bébé
C'est la nuit bébé
La nuit bébé
C'est le temps de se coucher

Dodo bébé
T'es fatigué
Fatigué
C'est le temps de se coucher

Tes toutous dorment et toi aussi
Tu dois dormir toute la nuit
Tu dors bébé
Tes yeux sont fermés
Tu dois rêver
Que c'est le temps de se coucher

Maman fait dodo

(3:38)

WORDS AND MUSIC
Connie Kaldor,
Carmen Campagne

Maman fait dodo
Papa fait dodo
Bébé fait dodo aussi
Bébé fait dodo pour la nuit

Do do
Fais dodo
Do do do

Mama wants to sleep
Daddy's fast asleep
Baby won't you close your eyes
Baby won't you beddy bye

Night night
Sleep tight
Mama loves you
Nighty night

Les chiens font dodo
Les chats font dodo
Bébé fait dodo aussi
Bébé fait dodo pour la nuit

The puppy down the stairs is asleep
The kitty on the chair is asleep
Baby won't you close your eyes
Baby won't you beddy bye

Ta poupée fait dodo
Ton ours fait dodo
Bébé fait dodo aussi
Bébé fait dodo pour la nuit

Dolly's gone to sleep
Teddy's gone to sleep
Baby won't you close your eyes
Baby won't you beddy bye

Berceuse pour Emanuel Reuben James

(2:06)

WORDS AND MUSIC
Edith Butler

Dors bien mon ange bleu
Ferme tes jolis yeux
Demain sera plus beau
Dors bien contre ma peau

Je n'ai rien à te donner
Qu'un peu d'amour
Un peu d'été
Je te raconterai
Comment dansent les poupées

Isabeau

(2:18)

TRADITIONAL, ARRANGEMENT
Carmen Campagne

All songs performed by CONNIE KALDOR and CARMEN CAMPAGNE Story CONNIE KALDOR
Illustrations BRIAN DEINES Record Producer DAN DONAHUE Artistic Director ROLAND STRINGER
Graphic Design STEPHAN LORTI, CHRISTIANE BEAULIEU Musicians CONNIE KALDOR piano,
keyboards, baby toys DAN DONAHUE guitar, keyboards, baby toys PAUL CAMPAGNE bass
MARILYN LERNER piano MICHEL LAVOIE piano

Vocals ALINE, SUZANNE, SOLANGE, PAUL, ANNETTE, and MICHELLE CAMPAGNE, DAN DONAHUE
Childrens' voices STÉPHANE CAMPAGNE-FORTIER, BENOIT CAMPAGNE FOREST, TRISTAN FORTIER-ALLAIN
Recorded by JOHN SCHRITT and DAN DONAHUE at RUST STUDIOS and mixed at FINUCAN STUDIOS
Mastered by TOBY GENDRON and PAUL CAMPAGNE at STUDIO KARISMA MONTANA

Thanks to Michel Lavoie, Aline Campagne, Solange Campagne, Michelle Fortier, Marguerite Campagne,
Paul Campagne, Nancy White, Ann Hepper, Leif Kaldor, Shirley Adam, Vern Bond, Louanne Beaucage, Ross Porter

Dedicated to Harold Kaldor – for all the lullabies he sang to put Connie to sleep

www.thesecretmountain.com

p 2005 FOLLE AVOINE PRODUCTIONS c 2005 Word of Mouth Music and Homestead Music
ISBN 2-923163-22-2. All rights reserved. No part of this book or recording may be reproduced or transmitted in any form or
by any means, electronic or mechanical, including photocopying, recording or by any information storage or retrieval system,
without permission in writing by the copyright holder. First printed in Hong Kong, China by Book Art Inc., Toronto.